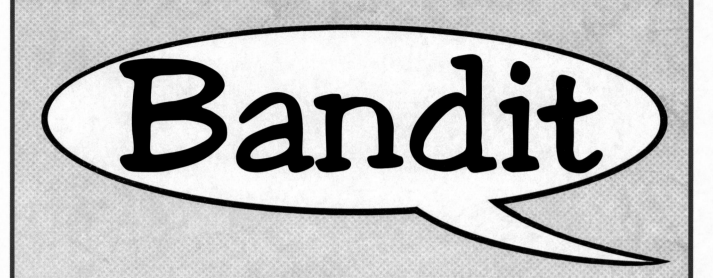

Bandit

by Karen Rostoker-Gruber

illustrated by Vincent Nguyen

Marshall Cavendish Children

Text copyright © 2008 by KRG Entertainment, LLC
Illustrations copyright © 2008 by Vincent Nguyen

All rights reserved
Marshall Cavendish Corporation
99 White Plains Road
Tarrytown, NY 10591
www.marshallcavendish.us/kids

Library of Congress Cataloging-in-Publication Data
Rostoker-Gruber, Karen.
Bandit / by Karen Rostoker-Gruber;
illustrated by Vincent Nguyen. — 1st ed.
p. cm.
Summary: When Bandit's family moves to a new house,
the cat runs away and returns to the only home he knows,
but after he is brought back, he understands that the new
house is now home.
ISBN 978-0-7614-5382-6
[1. Cats—Fiction. 2. Moving, Household—Fiction.]
I. Nguyen, Vincent, ill. II. Title.
PZ7.R72375Ban 2008
[E]—dc22
2007011720

The text of this book is set in Frutiger.
The illustrations are rendered in Graphite pencil/ink/watercolor and photoshop.
Book design by Vera Soki
Editor: Margery Cuyler

Printed in Malaysia
First edition
3 5 6 4

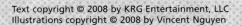

mc Marshall Cavendish
Children

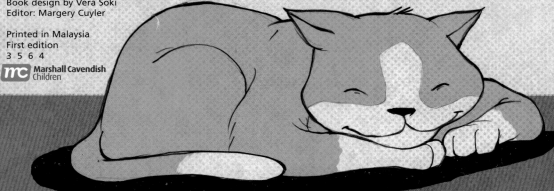

To Noah Nguyen
—V. N.
To Bandit, Donna, Daniel, and David, with hairballs!
And a special thanks to Margery Cuyler,
whose visionary ability is fur-st class!
—K. R-G.

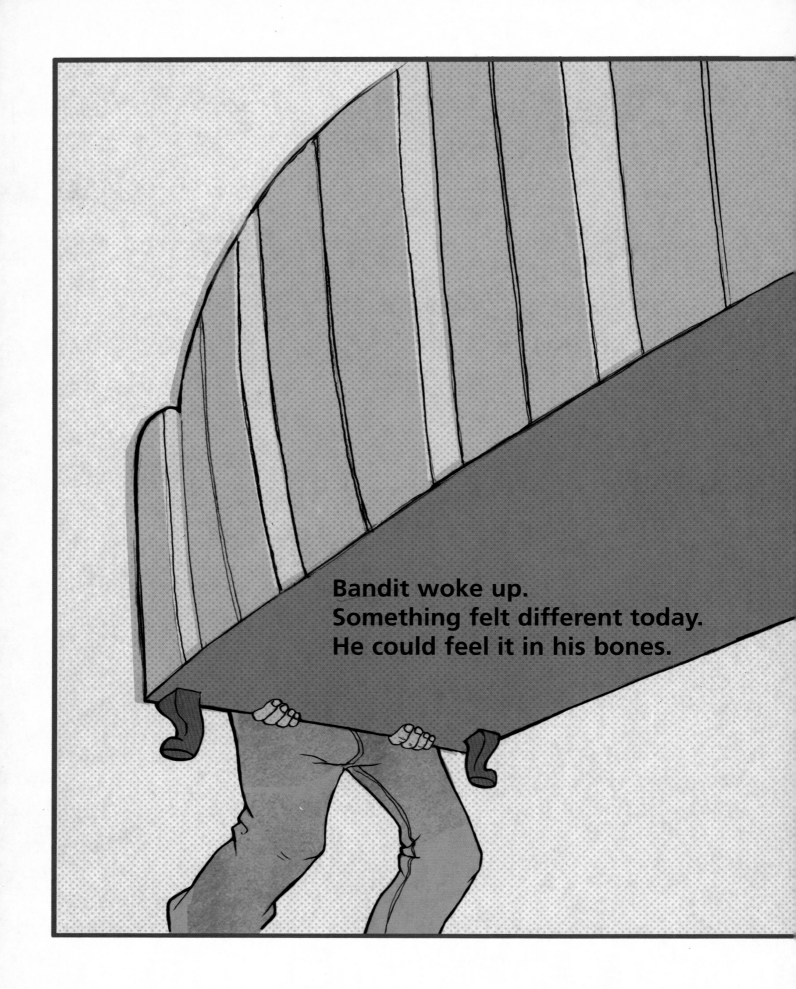

Bandit woke up.
Something felt different today.
He could feel it in his bones.

Suddenly, Michelle grabbed Bandit.

Bandit squirmed. Michelle held him tight.

Squeeze a hairball out of me, why don't you!

Michelle carried Bandit through the family room,

No toy basket?
No fuzzy mouse?
No blanket?
No bed?

down the hall,

and into the garage.
Michelle put Bandit in his cat carrier.

And off they drove down the driveway.

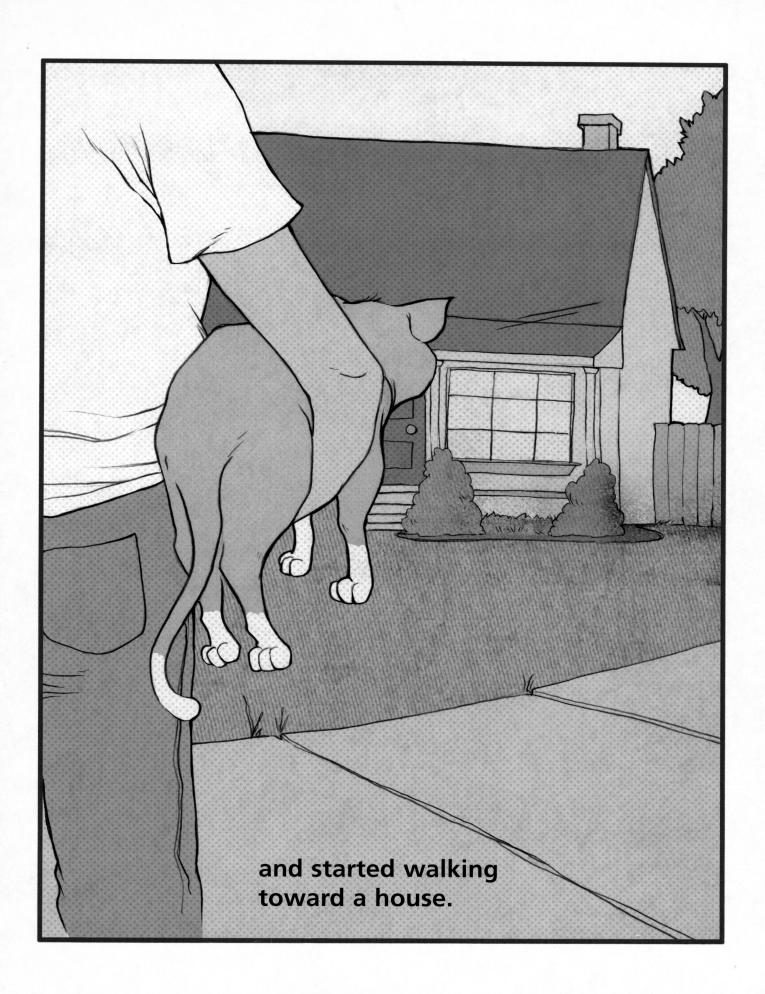

and started walking
toward a house.

Bandit squeezed through an open window,

ran down the driveway,

past a picket fence,

a pizza parlor,

a gas station,

and a bank.

He ran up
the driveway,

pushed through
the broken
screen door,

and headed
inside.

Bandit curled up on the soft carpeting in the sunny spot in the family room.
His favorite spot.
He slept like a kitten.

Home sweet home.

Suddenly, Bandit heard footsteps.

Michelle put Bandit back into his carrier.

And off they drove until Michelle stopped the car.

and the laundry room.

My litter box.
My food bowl.
TUNA! Purrrfect.

Bandit devoured the tuna.